This book is dedicated to my children and grandchildren. You are His Masterpiece. May your lives on this earth reflect the one who created you. You are my greatest blessings and I love you with all my heart.
Xoxo

Printed in the United States of America

First Printing, 2019

The Zany Adventures of
Zachary Bear

Meet
ZACH BEAR

By
Christi Beall Hurtak

Illustrated by
Joanna Garcia

This is the introduction to a series of adventures in the lives of an extraordinary family of bears. This beloved bear family is made up of:

Mommy Bear,

Daddy Bear,

and three brother bears named,

Zachary, Jacob, and Caleb.

Zachary, the oldest brother bear — we will call him Zach — is a bit different than his little brothers, but in many ways...

he is just like you.

How is Zach Bear different, you ask?
When Zach was just a baby bear,
Mommy Bear noticed he began

flapping his paws

and **moving his wrists**
again and again.

Mommy Bear decided to take Zach Bear to the doctor to find out
why he made this peculiar movement with his paws.

The doctor sent Zach Bear to the hospital to get tested so he could understand why Zach Bear moved his paws in this manner. Yes, Zach Bear makes awkward movements beyond his control, but in many ways...

he is just like you.

Finally, the doctor had answers for Zach's
Mommy and Daddy. He explained that
Zach had something called

AUTISM

When you have **autism,** your brain
works differently than most.

Autism can sometimes cause one or more parts of the brain to work exceptionally well. Zach is very good at doing math.

Yes, Zach Bear is better at math than most bears,
but in many ways...

he is just like you.

Zach Bear is thin, tall, handsome, and wears glasses.
His favorite color is red, and he loves to play games
on his iPawd.

For Zach Bear, every day is
a good hair day. He likes to
smile and laugh a lot.

He moves around quite a bit and has a hard time keeping still. He does something called "Stimming."

He flaps his paws, hops up and down, moves his wrists again and again, or spins around and around. Stimming is part of Zach's autism.

Yes, Zach often stims, but in many ways...

he is just like you.

Zach Bear enjoys watching doors open and close, jumping on his trampoline, riding on elevators (he likes to pretend he is in a time machine), turning lights off and on, looking at pictures in books, wrestling with Daddy Bear, and looking at walls.

A wall is just a wall to you, but when Zach looks at the wall, his brain may show him colors, numbers, letters, or beautiful pictures.

Yes, the way Zach Bear plays is different, but in many ways...

he is just like you.

When the doctor found out that Zach Bear had Autism, he gave him medicine in the form of something called "therapy."

Therapy will not make autism go away, but it helps Zach Bear talk better, listen better, learn better, and feel better.

Feeling better makes Zach a happy bear. Yes, Zach Bear has to learn in a different way, but in many ways...

he is just like you.

Playing with friends makes Zach Bear happy. Mommy Bear often takes Zach and his brothers on playdates. Zach's little brothers, Jake and Caleb, enjoy playing with their friends.

Sometimes they share their friends with their brother Zach because having autism makes it hard for him to make friends on his own.

Zach likes having friends. Yes, Zach Bear has a hard time making friends, but in many ways...

he is just like you.

Zach Bear wants friends and so do each of you.
The best way to make friends is by being kind.

We must be kind.

So when Zach Bear stims, acts differently, talks
differently, plays differently or learns differently,
you should not stare or laugh.

Try, instead, to understand that his autism makes
him different in all of these ways. Yes, Zach is
different, but just remember, in many ways...

Zach Bear is just like you.

We are all different in some ways and all alike in others. Some are tall, some are short, some are skinny, some like sports. Some can talk, some can swim. Some can walk and some cannot.

Some run fast, some run slow, some sing high, some sing low. Some like cold, some like hot. Some have autism and some do not. Some are dark, some are light, but ALL are precious in God's sight.

Yes, God made us ALL different, but God gave each of us a heart filled with His love.

Zach Bear loves his family and they love him. Loving and caring for each other makes Zach's family extraordinary.

God created all of us to be different and special, but He wants us to love each other the same.

Let's love one another.

Besides Zach's ability to do math well, he loves music.
Will you be Zach Bear's friend and sing this song with him?
(*Sung to the tune of "This Old Man."*)

God made me.

God made you.

We are different, yes, it's true.

But when we are kind and open up our hearts,

friendship grows right from the start!

Yes, God made Zach Bear different, but he wants friends,
JUST LIKE YOU!

Do you know someone with autism?

How do you know they have autism?

What can you do to be their friend?

The End

About the Author

My name is Christi Hurtak. I am a wife, a mother, and a grandmother. My oldest grandson, Zachary, was diagnosed with autism at the age of two. Since then I've learned the true meaning of walking by faith and not by sight. My daughter started a non-profit called Zach Speaks Inc. to provide autism families with financial support, encouragement and hope for their journey. Since becoming Zach's "Nonna" and being part of this foundation, I've gained knowledge and insight I hope to share through the real life experiences of our own autism journey with Zach, depicted in this book series as "Zach Bear."

Special thanks to Zach's therapists, Zach's teachers, and Zach Speaks Inc. board members.

About the Illustrator

Joanna Garcia is an illustrator, graphic designer, and entrepreneur. She obtained her B.S. in Graphic Design with a minor in Studio Art from Liberty University in 2015. She enjoys working in various mediums and styles in her artwork, from painting and sketching to digital illustrations.

Joanna and her husband, John, live in beautiful Lynchburg, VA with their two dogs, three guinea pigs, and one cat. A great deal of Joanna's inspiration comes from God's beautiful wildlife and nature.

COMING SOON TO A BOOKSTORE NEAR YOU:

Made in the USA
Columbia, SC
14 April 2023

14834807R00015